THE MAN WHO SOLD THE SHADE

a korean folk tale retold by vivian binnamin and illustrated by yumi heo

Macmillan
McGraw-Hill

New York   Farmington

One hot summer day long, long ago, a young man worked at the edge of a field. The sun burned like fire in the sky. Drops of sweat rolled down the man's face.

He was trying to repair a fence. He wiped his neck. He took a drink, but his throat still felt like sand. He could work no more. It was just too hot.

He looked across the field and saw a tree. Its great branches and green leaves began to swing in the hot breeze.

"Ah!" he said. "Shade!"

The tree grew outside the gate of a very big house. The man walked slowly to the tree. He sat down in the cool shade of its branches.

Soon the man was asleep. He dreamed of cool water in a stone fountain on a chilly day.

"Nice!" he said in his sleep.

"Not at all nice!" he heard someone say.

The man was startled. He sat up straight. "Who said that?" he asked.

Then he saw a man sitting under the other side of the tree. The man was resting on a pile of soft silk pillows. He wore very fine clothes. He looked very rich.

"*I* said it," answered the man. "How dare you! I'll bet you sneaked over here to sit in my shade!"

"*Your* shade?" asked the young man.

"Yes, *my* shade," said the rich man. "My great-great grandfather planted this tree. Now it belongs to me. And so does its shade."

"But this tree belongs to all of us," argued the young man.

"No!" said the other man. "It belongs to me. Only me."

Then the young man had an idea.

"So, you own this shade?" he asked.

"Yes," said the rich man.

"Will you sell the shade to me?" asked the young man.

The rich man laughed. How silly he is! he thought. He thinks he can buy the shade.

He turned to the young man.

"Of course," he said. "Just pay me three gold coins. Then this cool, refreshing shade will be all yours."

"Done!" said the young man. He reached into his pocket and paid the three coins.

The rich man walked away, laughing to himself.

As the day went on, the shade grew longer. It grew across the grass and onto the sidewalk. Soon it reached past the grand gate and into the yard of the big house. The young man followed it. Then he lay down in the rich man's yard.

The rich man stormed out of his house.

"Get out of my yard," he yelled. "What are you doing here?"

"I'm just lying in my shade," said the young man.

The rich man growled. He glared at the man. Then he turned and walked back into his house.

Later the shade crept onto the rich man's porch. The young man followed it. Then it moved through the windows and into the big house. The young man opened the door and walked in.

"Get out!" yelled the rich man. "This is my house!"

"And this is my shade," said the young man, calmly.

"I'll give you back the three gold coins," offered the rich man.

"No, thank you," said the young man.

"I'LL GIVE YOU TEN COINS," yelled the rich man.

"No, thank you," said the young man politely.

As the sun went down, the shadows disappeared. Then the young man went home.

But the next day was sunny, and he came back. This time he brought his friends. They sat on the rich man's porch, talking and laughing.

The rich man could stand it no longer. He raced outside with a big bag of gold coins.

"Please," he begged. "Let me buy back my shade. I will pay you twenty gold coins."

"No, thank you," said the young man.

"Fifty!" offered the rich man.

"No, thank you," said the man again.

The rich man took a deep breath. "ALL RIGHT," he yelled. "TAKE ONE HUNDRED GOLD COINS!"

The young man took the coins. He and his friends left the house and never came back.

With the coins, the man bought his own house. Two great trees grew around it. His porch was always shady and cool. The young man often sat there with his friends . . . talking about the day he sold the shade for one hundred gold coins.